WILD ABOUT ANIMALS

I0886449

# ALLIGATORS

By Martha London

Kaleidoscope
Minneapolis, MN

BIGFOOT BOOKS

**The Quest for Discovery Never Ends**

*This edition first published in 2020 by Kaleidoscope Publishing, Inc.*

*No part of this publication may be reproduced in whole or in part without written permission of the publisher.*

*For information regarding permission, write to*
*Kaleidoscope Publishing, Inc.*
*6012 Blue Circle Drive*
*Minnetonka, MN 55343*

*Library of Congress Control Number*
*2019938721*

*ISBN*
*978-1-64519-000-4 (library bound)*
*978-1-64494-242-0 (paperback)*
*978-1-64519-100-1 (ebook)*

*Text copyright © 2020 by Kaleidoscope Publishing, Inc. All-Star Sports, Bigfoot Books, and associated logos are trademarks and/or registered trademarks of Kaleidoscope Publishing, Inc.*

*Printed in the United States of America.*

FIND ME IF YOU CAN!

**Bigfoot lurks within one of the images in this book. It's up to you to find him!**

# TABLE OF CONTENTS

CHAPTER 1

# Swallow Whole

The raccoon taking a drink doesn't know it's in danger. Hidden in the tall grass near shore is an alligator. It's dark out. The Louisiana night is **humid**. On the surface, the lake is calm. Everything is quiet. Only the moon reflects off the water.

The alligator is patient. He is an **ambush** predator. If the grass weren't here, it wouldn't matter. He can hold his breath for over an hour. Underwater, he can watch the shoreline. When the perfect meal comes, he attacks. This alligator is the biggest in the lake. He can take on big mammals like this raccoon.

*Alligators hide under the water to surprise the animals they hunt.*

The water is a couple feet deep. In the water, the alligator's tail sinks down. It almost touches the muddy bottom. The raccoon is still at the shore. Slowly, the alligator tenses his muscles. He's getting ready. Just a couple more seconds.

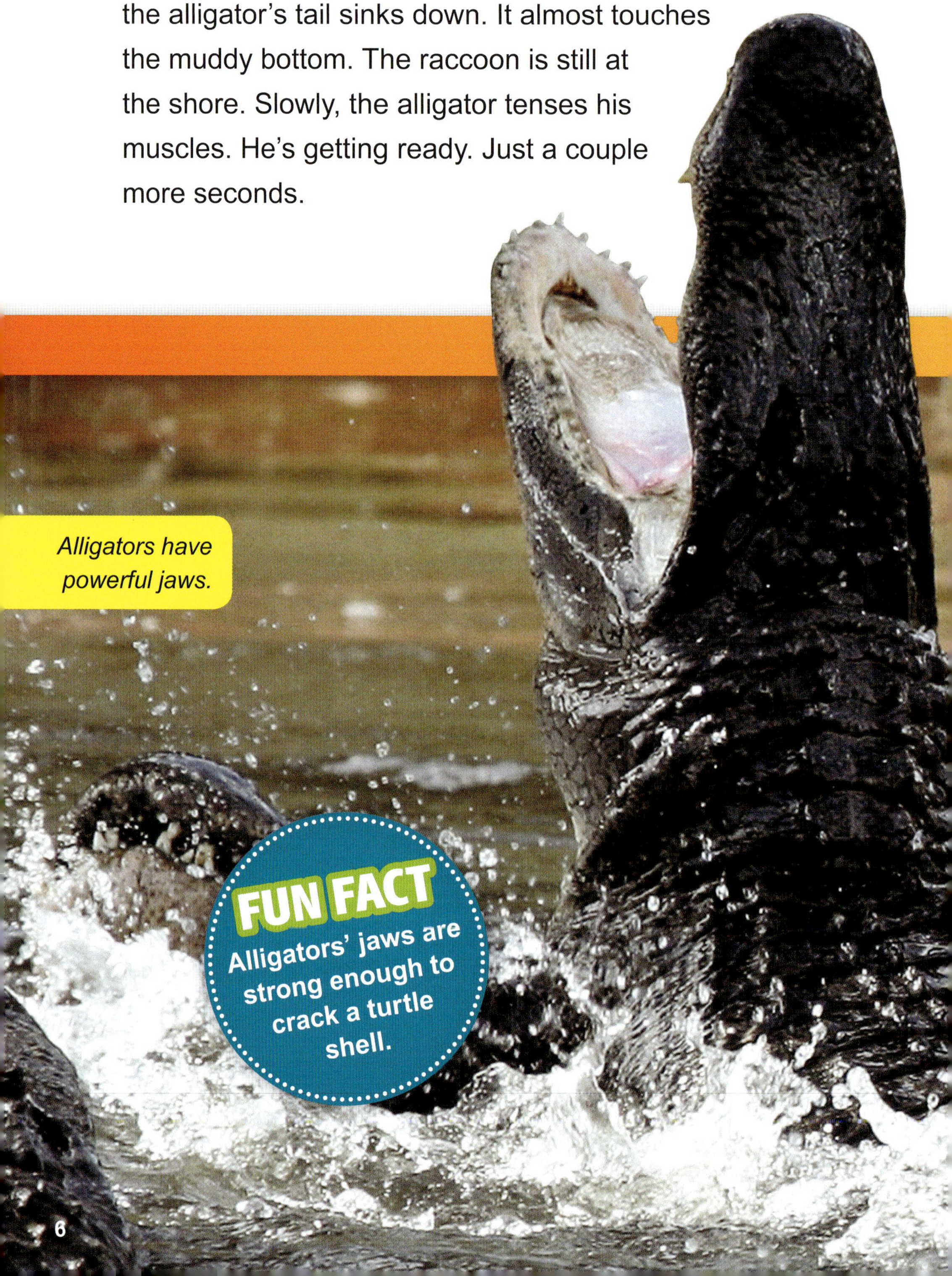

*Alligators have powerful jaws.*

**FUN FACT**
Alligators' jaws are strong enough to crack a turtle shell.

Bam! The alligator shoots out of the water. His powerful tail swings. He opens his mouth wide. Water splashes everywhere. When the mud and water settle, the raccoon isn't on shore anymore. It didn't get away. The alligator caught it in his strong jaws. He can crush bones easily. His teeth are as sharp as knives.

Alligators live in swamps.

But the alligator can't chew. This meal is too big for him to swallow all at once. He needs smaller pieces. With the raccoon in his mouth, he throws his head back and forth. His sharp teeth tear smaller pieces off. The alligator swallows the pieces whole. Bones are no problem for him. He eats those, too. Nothing goes to waste.

After his dinner, the alligator swims to shore. He digests food slowly. He won't need to eat for a couple days now. But if something comes along, he won't waste an opportunity.

CHAPTER 2

# Silent Predator

The alligator's eyes and snout are the only part visible above the water. Her body floats beneath the surface. She lives in a swamp. The water is dark and cloudy. The alligator blends in perfectly. She is dark gray. Pieces of algae stick to her head. Her head looks like a branch in the water. It's hard for **prey** to see her. She blends in.

*Alligators blend into the water.*

**FUN FACT**
There are only two species of alligator: American alligators and Chinese alligators.

Right now, she isn't hunting. Her feet hang at her side in the water. She has long nails. They are good for digging holes. She'll need them when she lays her eggs.

Her long, powerful tail rests below the water. When she needs to move quickly, her tail is the perfect tool. She can swim as fast as 20 miles per hour (32 km/h).

# PARTS OF AN ALLIGATOR

This alligator is big. She is old. She's been in this swamp for thirty years. Now she's one of the biggest alligators around. She's over 8 feet (2.4 m) long.

## CROCODILES VS. ALLIGATORS

**Alligators and crocodiles are part of the same family. They have many similar features. Both spend most of their time in the water. They are large predators. But alligators are different from their cousins. Alligators have round snouts. Crocodile snouts are more pointed. Alligators are also smaller and darker. Alligators and crocodiles mostly don't live in the same habitats. However, both alligators and crocodiles live in the southern tip of Florida.**

*New teeth will grow in if an alligator loses one.*

She can eat pretty much any prey she finds. Her jaws are very powerful. Sharp teeth line her mouth. When one of her eighty teeth falls out, a new one comes in. By now, she's had more than one thousand new teeth.

The alligator cruises through the water. After a few hours, she climbs onto shore. Alligators are **ectothermic**. She needs the heat of the sun to warm herself. Her legs are short. This makes it hard for her to move quickly on land. She usually only comes on land to sun herself and lay her eggs in the spring.

*Alligators need to heat up in the sun.*

## CHAPTER 3

# At Home in the Water

It's dark inside the egg. The baby alligator is outgrowing his home. But there is a lot of dirt above him. He and his siblings start chirping. They are calling to their mother. She needs to come help them. She hears the babies call.

She comes to the nest. The alligator uses her snout and feet to uncover the eggs. The baby alligators hatch from their shells. Their mother helps them to the shallow water.

**FUN FACT**

**The temperature of the egg in the nest determines whether a baby will be male or female.**

*Baby alligators hatch from eggs.*

*Baby alligators stay with their mothers for a few years.*

The Florida sun is hot in August. The baby hunts for bugs with his brothers and sisters. He knows his mother is close by. But it's still dangerous. Birds and larger animals might try to eat him. He stays hidden in tall grass along the shoreline. If a predator comes around, he calls to his mother. She rushes in to protect her babies. The little hatchling will stay close to his mother for a couple years.

The alligator will go to a new home when he's big enough. He'll stay close if there's food nearby. But if not, he might travel many miles to find a new home. He looks for calm water. Ponds and swamps are the best locations. There are lots of places to hide there.

# Where Do Alligators Live?

The alligator is bigger than he was. He moved away from his nest and lives on his own. He can eat birds now, but only if they come near the water. The alligator doesn't like working too hard. He prefers easy meals. That's why he eats mostly fish and frogs. They're easy to catch. They practically swim into his mouth.

# PEOPLE AND ALLIGATORS LIVING TOGETHER

Alligators go where there is water and food. Unfortunately, that sometimes puts them in the same place as people. Alligators are found on golf courses. They even end up in people's pools. Large alligators can be dangerous to people. Pets and children are especially at risk. Police will catch an alligator. They will bring it to a new home away from people.

*Baby alligators hunt with their brothers and sisters.*

CHAPTER 4

# Top of the Food Chain

In the **Everglades**, this alligator is king. The area is part of a park, so things are quiet here. He's 15 feet (4.6 m) long. His jaw could snap a turtle shell. He doesn't have to worry about predators. When he was young, he had to be careful. Larger alligators were dangerous. But he was smart. He found a home with fewer alligators. This guy is at the top of the food chain.

**FUN FACT**
**The name alligator comes from the Spanish "el legarto," meaning "the lizard."**

*Many alligators live in Everglades National Park in Florida.*

But his skin is valuable. People enjoy eating his meat. Before humans made rules, he would have been killed. His kind were almost hunted to **extinction**.

Now, though, he is protected. So is his home. Very few alligators in the wild are killed by people. Officials let people hunt alligators only once a year. This alligator tries to stay far away. He doesn't like the loud bang from the guns. It scares away the fish.

## *HOW BIG ARE*

# ALLIGATORS?

**American alligators can grow up to 15 FEET (4.6 M) long!**

*This alligator is in a zoo. Zoos give people the chance to learn about alligators.*

The humans have strict rules. The alligator's habitat is protected. People can't drain the water. They can't build golf courses and houses. He can live in peace.

His species isn't **endangered** anymore. But sometimes trash still gets in his home. Plastic bags and old bottles litter the shore. Sometimes he attacks trash instead of animals. The plastic tastes bad. Broken glass has cut the pad of his foot.

People come every once in a while and take the trash away. The alligator likes that. His home is clean and more animals come around. People are able to watch the alligator in his home. Scientists study alligators in the wild. They learn more and more. Scientists teach people how to live with alligators. People don't have to compete with alligators.

**FUN FACT**
An alligator named Mr. Stubbs learned to swim with a **prosthetic** tail.

*Pollution hurts alligators. They eat trash thinking it's food.*

# BEYOND THE BOOK

After reading the book, it's time to think about what you learned. Try the following exercises to jumpstart your ideas.

## THINK

**DIFFERENT SOURCES.** Think about what types of sources you could find on alligators. What could you find in an encyclopedia? What could you learn at a zoo? What about an interview with a scientist? How could each of the sources be useful in its own way?

## CREATE

**SHARPEN YOUR RESEARCH SKILLS.** Everglades National Park in Florida is an important habitat for many alligators. Where could you go in the library to find more information about this habitat? Who could you talk to who might know more? Create a research plan. Write a paragraph about your next steps.

## SHARE

**SUM IT UP.** Write one paragraph summarizing the important points from this book. Make sure it's in your own words. Don't just copy what is in the text. Share the paragraph with a classmate. Does your classmate have any comments about the summary? Do they have additional questions about alligators?

## GROW

**REAL-LIFE RESEARCH.** What places could you visit to learn more about alligators? What other things could you learn while you were there?

# RESEARCH NINJA

Visit www.ninjaresearcher.com/0004 to learn how to take your research skills and book report writing to the next level!

## RESEARCH

**DIGITAL LITERACY TOOLS**

### SEARCH LIKE A PRO
Learn about how to use search engines to find useful websites.

### FACT OR FAKE?
Discover how you can tell a trusted website from an untrustworthy resource.

### TEXT DETECTIVE
Explore how to zero in on the information you need most.

### SHOW YOUR WORK
Research responsibly—learn how to cite sources.

## WRITE

### GET TO THE POINT
Learn how to express your main ideas.

### PLAN OF ATTACK
Learn prewriting exercises and create an outline.

**DOWNLOADABLE REPORT FORMS**

# Further Resources

## BOOKS

Hamalainen, Karina. *Everglades*. Scholastic, 2019.

Mattern, Joanne. *Alligators and Crocodiles*. Red Chair Press, 2017.

O'Brien, Cynthia. *Bringing Back the American Alligator*. Crabtree Publishing, 2019.

## WEBSITES

Factsurfer.com gives you a safe, fun way to find more information.

1. Go to www.factsurfer.com.
2. Enter "Alligators" into the search box and click .
3. Select your book cover to see a list of related websites.

# Glossary

**ambush:** An ambush is a surprise attack. The alligator waited to ambush his prey.

**ectothermic:** An animal that is ectothermic needs to heat up in the sun. Alligators are ectothermic.

**endangered:** A species is endangered when its population in the wild is very low. Alligators are no longer endangered.

**Everglades:** Everglades is a national park in Florida. Alligators, manatees, and many other animals live in Everglades National Park.

**extinction:** Extinction is when every animal of a species dies. Alligators came back from the brink of extinction.

**habitats:** Habitats are places where animals live. Alligators and crocodiles usually live in different habitats.

**humid:** Humid air is damp and full of moisture. Florida's weather is hot and humid.

**prey:** Prey is an animal that another animal eats. Fish and frogs are perfect prey for alligators.

**prosthetic:** A prosthetic replaces a body part that is missing. Mr. Stubbs lost his tail, but he learned to swim with a new prosthetic tail.

# Index



## PHOTO CREDITS

The images in this book are reproduced through the courtesy of: Roberto La Rosa/Shutterstock Images, front cover; Heiko Kiera/Shutterstock Images, pp. 3, 13; underworld111/iStockphoto, p. 4; Ira Mark Rappaport/Shutterstock Images, pp. 4–5; mark higgins/Shutterstock Images, pp. 6–7; LagunaticPhoto/Shutterstock Images, pp. 8–9; Eric Isselee/Shutterstock Images, pp. 9, 24–25; emin kuliyev/Shutterstock Images, pp. 10–11; Keith Michael Taylor/Shutterstock Images, p. 12; Ekaterina Kamenetsky/Shutterstock Images, pp. 14–15; DimaSid/Shutterstock Images, pp. 16–17; IrinaK/Shutterstock Images, p. 17; Orhan Cam/Shutterstock Images, pp. 18–19; tonyz20/Shutterstock Images, p. 19; Red Line Editorial, p. 20; Steve Byland/Shutterstock Images, p. 21; Mark_Kostich/Shutterstock Images, p. 22–23; Chipmunk131/Shutterstock Images, p. 25; meunierd/Shutterstock Images, p. 26; Tory Kallman/Shutterstock Images, p. 27; Songquan Deng/Shutterstock Images, p. 30.

## ABOUT THE AUTHOR

Martha London is a Twin Cities–based writer. She is a lover of all animals.